Praise for *BARROW* and other works :

"Tombs are my books. Bones are my poems. Skin my page. Breath, my ink Read like blood, my essential kin," the poet says. In *Barrow*, Bryan Thao Worra witnesses language and the world organizing each other. He excavates the complexities of perception—a syntax of self-definition animating a semantics of cultural criticism. Myth, popular culture, philosophy, music, science, lives, deaths, real talk, passion, longing, and an appetite for juxtaposition fill, fold, and digest his universe. But this is not "language poetry"—Worra's puns, neologisms and allusions are not goals, but road signs. His poetry is a searching and empathetic inversion of Philip K. Dick's brilliant paranoia. Some advice: read *Barrow* not as separate poems, but as a whole, a rough quilt of reality and imagination that will warm your soul.

—John Calvin Rezmerski, poet and editor

Bryan Thao Worra's *Barrow* is a rich poetic fugue, building and turning into itself, an echo and song guiding the reader through questions of war, home, death, and outer space. Worra's insistence on finding definition in forgotten lore, displaced heritage, and unimagined possibilities is a journey well worth traveling, not for the sake of simple answers but for a true exploration into the imagination of a tremendous writer.

- Oscar Bermeo, author of *Anywhere Avenue* and *Palimpsest*

"A cross between Rilke and Pink Floyd, genetically enhanced with scenes from Forbidden Planet, left to grow in a beaker, using steaming pho as its nutrient base. *Barrow* comes to life and crawls across the laboratory floor, stands up on multiple legs, and challenges the universe. This is more than pretty words, more than one man's trip around the world, more than his considerable talent. *Barrow* asks questions we are afraid to ask when we're sober, and reveals answers we have hidden away. This is a testament."

—Britt Fleming, editor of *Northography*

"Bryan Thao Worra's work is a vital and essential part of the story of Laotian American literature. It raises our bar of expectations and assures us of many amazing works yet to come."

—Saymoukda Vongsay, author of *No Regrets*

"Poetry often tends to make me go, "Hmm," "Oh," or "That's nice." Bryan Thao Worra's poetry makes me laugh, flip back the page to consider that last bit again, or cry out, "What?" (and I mean that in a good way). On the Other Side of the Eye" is at once other-worldly and yet strangely familiar, as though I have already asked and explored those questions in a waking dream."

-Ji In Lugtu, cultural critic, *Twice The Rice*

"Fun, witty, universal yet oddly intimate, Bryan Thao Worra pulls his readers into alien yet familiar areas of the human experience. From its pages, On the Other Side of the Eye whispers to our inner alien with a challenge to recognize the monster within all of us. Yet, far from being judgmental or conclusive, he narrates with the voice of a seeker whose infectious curiosity reminds us that the world is infinitely full of wonder."

-Sumeia, cultural critic, *Ethnically Incorrect Daughter*

"I've been reading this striking book [*On the Other Side of the Eye*] over the past two months, every day on the train, making my way through the layers of writing and my own thoughts. It's a remarkable collection, full of lonesome, searching and speculative songs as if Hank Williams contemplated Lovecraft instead of love…
…Thao Worra gives it to you together to show you all that is broken and beautiful in this terrible world."

-Ed Lin, author of *Waylaid* and *This Is A Bust!*

"Bryan Thao Worra's first collection, ON THE OTHER SIDE OF THE EYE, clearly distinguishes itself as apart yet mixed, full of strange devices and exquisitely memorable constructs that leaves the reader immersed in wonder… ON THE OTHER SIDE OF THE EYE is rife with pop culture references, yet underlying all is a universal truth: that poetry speaks of the human experience and all that it contains."

-James Roberts, *Mad Poets of Terra*, Spring 2008

"…Thao Worra, a first generation Laotian-American, finds his own voice in this collection, darkly humorous and intelligent, scraping together cultural mythologies and dicing them up with scenes of personal experience. In his best pieces he has a unique style where East and West get thrown together like bacon and eggs."

-Whistling Shade, 2004

BARROW

*Poems by
Bryan Thao Worra*

Sam's Dot Publishing

Copyright © 2009

All rights reserved. No part of this book may be reproduced in any form or by any electronic or mechanical means, including information storage and retrieval systems-except in the case of brief quotations embodied in critical articles or reviews-without permission in writing from its author.

Cover by Vongduane Manivong (www.vongduane.com)

Published and bound in the United States of America

Dedicated to
The Different Ones.

Foreword

by Dr. Nnedi Okorafor

I was a witch looking for a gift for a wizard.

I traveled deep into a shaded market while on my trip to Nigeria looking for it. After an hour of searching, the strange palm-sized, black wooden mask instantly caught my eye. It practically had Bryan Thao Worra's name written on it. The mask had three pairs of eyes; whatever deity, spirit or creature it was could probably see into the past, present and future. It was crafted by a man of the Fulani tribe, a nomadic people known for their poetry, magic formulas, stories, legends, and riddles.

The mask's creator, however, was absent (I had to buy it from his assistant). This dark market was in the city of Lagos- take away the "g" from "Lagos" and you get "Laos". As the guild navigator in Frank Herbert's Dune said, "I see plans within plans." Within this mask I saw…Well, that's a tale for another time. This mask now sits on Bryan's mantle, as it was meant to.

I met the Laotian-American wizard known as Bryan Thao Worra some years ago at Think Galacticon, a Midwestern convention for leftists who seek to discuss politics and speculative fiction. One of the first things I noticed about him was his audacity. He always had the nerve to say those inflammatory things I was thinking but never had the guts to utter. I later understood that he was one of those literary magic men who laces his language with booby traps, mazes, and… rabbit holes.

When I read his poetry, I think of a classic moment from Lewis Carroll's *Through the Looking Glass*:

> 'The time has come,' the Walrus said,
> 'To talk of many things:
> Of shoes—and ships—and sealing wax –
> Of cabbages–and kings—
> And why the sea is boiling hot –
> And whether pigs have wings.'

And have no doubt, in any of his books, he'll talk of many things.

One of the hallmarks of Bryan's writing is his cosmopolitan globe-trotting: You'll run into ancient history, pop culture, 50s B-movies, puzzles and hidden messages, nods to James Joyce and Apocalypse Now and more than a few slumming gods and goddesses and spiders. And amid <u>all</u> of that chaos, you'll find him spinning a thread between them <u>all</u>.

In these pages words have many meanings, many readings. You'll walk away with something just from a surface reading, but there's always something that lingers and rewards you when you look deeper, under the skin, into the dark.

Dr. Nnedi Okorafor is the award-winning author of the novels *Zahrah the Windseeker*, *The Shadow Speaker* and *Who Fears Death*. You can visit her online at www.nnedi.com.

Barrow: n. 1) A large mound of earth or stones placed over a burial site. 2) A wheelbarrow. 3) A pig who has been castrated before reaching sexual maturity. 4) A count of forty threads in the warp or chain of woolen cloth. 5) An old lunar crater located near the northern limb of the Moon. It lies between Goldschmidt crater to the northwest and the irregular Meton crater formation. 6) To be determined.

I.

Here, the River Haunt.
Temporary Passages
Anger
Today's Special at the Shuang Cheng
Still Life
The Artist and War (Fragments)
Fieldcraft
Tetragrammaton
To an Old Tune
Mythology
A Hmong Goodbye
A Vision of Invasion
My Autopsy, Thank You
Preguntas
What Tomorrow Takes Away
The Hymn of Stones

II.

XXII
Vocabularies
Chartreuse
Homunculus
Genesis 2020
The Dancer Introduces One of His Aspects
Riding the 16
Labyrinth

III.

To the Petshop Gecko
Modern Life
Sprawl
The Big G.
Cobra
Legion
Zhu Bajie

IV.

Minotaur
Reconsidering Gordian
For the Friend Who Will Never Read This
Libertree
Lady Xoc
Everything Belongs to the Spider
Severances
Loom
Shuttle
Tie: A Knot's Perspective

V.

Acts of Confession
A Little Bat
Mischief in the Heavens
The Spirit Catches You and You Get Body Slammed
Dragon Jazz
Tempus Fugit
Soap
Fnord
The Fifth Wish
Insomniacafe
Swallowing the Moon
Hey Einstein
Lunacy

VI.

How To Build A Boat

Barrow: *n. A large mound of earth or stones placed over a burial site.*

"What did the victims matter who the machine destroyed on its way? Wasn't it bound for the future, heedless of spilt blood? With no human hand to guide it through the night, it roared onward, a blind and deaf beast let loose amid death and destruction, laden with cannon-fodder, those soldiers already silly with fatigue, drunk and bawling."

-Emile Zola, La Bête Humaine

Here, the River Haunt.

Bodies of students young despair:
An artist, the whispered, teeth and hair.
Some spectral digits clasp at flags and tear.
Yon wave and pavement witness near
Your campus of dreams, the shade and clear
To see such windy seas our clashing forms are from,
Fathom foam and phantom, our eerie erring ear.

What unwise winding butcher Time will cease and pare, without peer.

Temporary Passages

Gone soon, the Three Gorges of the Yellow River,
     chipped Egyptian colossi,
                          famed as they are
and in a flash, the anonymous man struck by a bus
on his way
                                  to work.
To say nothing of the modern musician for whom
such a term is loosely,
         generously applied.

Laugh, Shelly, at these hieroglyphs
as your own tongue decays,

    And Bryan can
    barely remember
    the beautiful song
    of doomed sparrows
    outside his chamber
    at the Hotel Du Square
    after just five minutes!
    How can he expect the heavens to remember
    these tiny words he insists on writing
            for every young girl
      who's afraid of

                     death?

Anger

Coiling within, this? Not the face I would show you.
The roar beneath wires, the roar hushed by white noise
Blanketing the land.

Shadows, night's exiles: "Go fugitive in the streets."

Skylines punctuate sentences of geography with
Incessant luminescence.
Our world is aglow. There is no time
When all of the citizens of our city

> Are asleep at once anymore.

> I learned to despise without passion.
> I rear up, a dragon.
> I open my jaw, a tiger defending the last hour men drink.

I cleave open the heart of my lovers that I may rest in them,
Nestled against the storm.

> My dispositions:
> Collated.
> Codified response, taking flight through banks
> Of predictable information for the sake of cool conformity,
> Instead of soaring

> Across landscapes wired solely by
> Rivers and the silence.

Today's Special at the Shuang Cheng

Coated in caramelized spice:
The suckers of a squid tentacle
diced into impotence
between my chopsticks
and baked.

They once clutched
at an ocean
writhing with life,
clasping dearly to each precious bite.

What will worms use
to hold my bony hands
if I don't let my family
throw me into the
sea ,

a handful of dust
with a hint of squid flavoring.

Still Life

It's a grave thing.
Absent the living.
Objects arrayed.
Pose in light and shade,
Suggest meaning for the animate remaining.

Here a painting,
A sketch or a garden of stones,
A quenched flame,
A planet on the last day of all beings
Now silent, no more transforming

    Amid the novas and nebulae.

With finality,
Every human to earth returns.

        Free.

        Creatures of plots.

The Artist and War (Fragments)

I.

Hung across from *Abstract Nature*
    : bellicose icons silent on :
The wars of Asia.

      My love wonders:
  Too painful to face
      Still? Or too familiar
  To require comment on?

II.

A video game designer in Virginia
Told me: war games on
Vietnam just don't sell, let alone those
Of secret wars or killing fields. Besides,
What karma could such amusements bring?

III.

By the *"Massacre of the Civilian Population
In Timizoara, Romania"*
I remember :

    The *"Winged Victory of Samothrace"*
A decapitated beauty whose severed neck

Speaks more truth of victory's real price
    Than those snarling stone lips long since stolen
For the conquering wheel.

Fieldcraft

Don't wear pistols on the field.
They'll think you're in charge,
Sniper bait.

Don't stand by the sucker
Strapped to the radio.
The guy calling for help

Is always trouble,
Bringing his buddies and
Beaucoup Boom Boom.

Hence, he's a real lead magnet,
As bad as it gets.

Go ahead and take point.
They want the guys behind you,
Chatting in the jungle with
Their bad aftershave

Giving them away like candy at the carnival,
Loud as a half-filled olive green canteen
Of stale water writhing with liver flukes.

Duck and cover
When the skies fill with nukes.
Don't breathe too hard if you get a whiff of
Something funky in the air like Satan's Tang.

Don't scream. Don't run. Watch your step at all times.
A mine could be anywhere,
Or you could die impaled like a vampire
On some bamboo skewer

For a minor hill
That doesn't get a name
Only a number.

Tetragrammaton

Among the monotheists: We are children of the Word,
From the very first second in which light came to Be,
Before a witness was, a single eye blinked.

A mystic in New York will tell you:
He believes in the 72-syllable secret name of God,
Even more than the genome we spent half his lifetime collating.

"God is certain, chemicals are not," he says confidently,
His shallow face lit by a thin scented candle from India,
His great wall of used books behind him filled with unread passages.

In September in the basement of Qwest's center:
Young Khadra confirms for me
She knows all of the sacred names of Allah and still believes

As our world crashes.
Her faith, unfashionable, my words, so small.

We, laid off in October:
Barely warning or fanfare
While Russians remember
Their Great Revolution for Red Square.

Only a handful still revere the State's blushing face
Twisting on giant banners in the cold Muscovite wind.

"My name means 'Green'" Khadra says, waiting for our bus one last time.
"And it's true, I come from a nation of poets. Is yours such a place?"

I do not know how to reply, distracted. Thinking
How hard it was, to imagine

That single perfect word by which a universe might be made,

Watching a nearby wild flower and a monarch butterfly
Who both seem so free without these questions:
Destined to die with the first winter frost

But still enjoying their time together.

To an Old Tune

I didn't start a poet.
Did all to stall it.
Called it a hobby, a summer cloud,
An Iowa rainbow.

It's water in a floating world
Crammed with people who are
Secretly 3/4ths ocean wave and
1/4th black stardust.

What I really wanted to be is
Too embarrassing to tell,
But if I go to hell now,
It's what I'll be doing
For the rest of my afterlife.

Mythologies

Donna means woman.
Bella means beautiful.
The two together are a deadly poison,
The kissing cousin of nightshade.

Elsewhere, sure as hemlock for
The throats of sages in their curious passage,
Corrupting the freest

      The Void

Howls, a white wolf for your bones,
Who hopes to make soup for the devil
Beside the river stones

Like curveless Pandora for her Titan
Lurking by the curling vine.

A Hmong Goodbye

I'm playing Scrabble
At the funeral on English Street
With idle children

Who already know: Death
Took forever out here.
Meanwhile, the old men of St. Paul

Curse each other's shifting fortunes
In their coarse card games
As forty ounce bottles slowly

Slide down throats to swollen bellies
The hue of amber and rice.

Tears are reserved for the women
In the next room among suspended drums

And droning horns of bamboo and gourd
Singing a dry roadmap to the next world.

Incense, hairspray and perfume
Permeate the waxy parlor

While a young boy wonders if it is true
You need special shoes when walking
Over the Land of Fuzzy Caterpillars towards Heaven
With a split soul.

My opponents look up accusingly,
Scattering tiles to every corner,
Running off to play

Other games instead,
Minute mouths mocking
The word EXTINCT,

Pronouncing it fraud.

A Vision of Invasion

Someday I expect
Egypt will launch

A surprise attack
And pry the hands off Big Ben.

Whisk away the antenna of the Eiffel Tower
And carry off the rubble of the House of Commons.

Students of archaeology will travel from far abroad
To witness a history reclaimed and preserved

Beneath an unflinching sun
While Euromania sweeps the country

And bad copies of Spice Girl photos are sold to decorate tacky homes.
Oh, what do you care, poet?

They don't even bother trying to preserve your heart.
My poems must serve as my canopic jars.

Wight

Long the nail iron in
What's cleft from time, the body seasoning.
Clamber, clatter, silence seeker.

Reek of all the morrows who round us ring!

I know well both sides our craven slab
So lustily devouring
We clay scrabbles, we clawed things.

>Tombs are my books.
>Bones are my poems.
>Skin my page.
>Breath, my ink
>Read like blood, my essential kin.
>Yesterday, my many spines.
>
>The rags? Nothings after all.

My Autopsy, Thank You

In the hollows of my chest
Between my heart and other assorted pieces of viscera,
Was there ever really enough room for my soul?

When the scalpels plunge into me,
Dancing between veins and arteries and bone,
Will the surgeons laugh, or speak in monotone?

Am I just my flesh,
A chemical soup or a sausage sack?

Is my soul everything between the spaces of my vitals,
Or is it these things too? Or none of the above?

Please doctor, as you poke and pry,
If you should find any answers for me,

Whisper them in what's left of my ears
Or carve them next to: RETURN TO SENDER

With my name attached,

Using your stainless steel razor sharp letter openers.
Feel free to rummage through and push aside
Whatever's in the way.

As for the fluids that I drip on you,
I can't help it anymore.

I'd say I'm sorry, but how can I,

If my fears and loves and cares were trapped inside
This mortal heart,
When it was blown out of the cavity of my chest

    Into the streets for strangers to slip in?

Preguntas

If Neruda asks
This cloudy question
He is a poet, undisputed

A noble master of letters

When these words pass through
A Zen abbot's lips
We hear a cryptic koan, impossible

A riddle to defy attachment

If lustrous Hồ Xuân Hương idly toys
With this conundrum upon
Her pliant ink-stained lap, inscrutable

She becomes an oral tradition
For romantic schoolboys in old Saigon

Should I dare repeat
Any of this aloud while still alive,
I am a fool to be buried in the cold grooves
Of Saint Cloud.

Now, how fair is that?

What Tomorrow Takes Away

On a good day,
The feeling of
Something left undone,
Nagging like Mrs. Tolstoy
On your deathbed in Astapovo.

On a bad day,
The feeling that
Something has been
Accomplished
Like Mr. Tolstoy's last period
For a book called War and Peace.

I wish we weren't so obsessed with hope.
Because in a good world,
We wouldn't need it at all.

The Hymn of Stones

Learn something true of the world
And you'll never want.

Others will foist and prod,
Chafe and stamp, object.

Hold it within, it becomes a treasure,
Your tomb.

Share it, and your hands become empty.
You truly live.

Learn of the world's wants
And you'll become some thing of nevers:

Want to learn of the world?
Some things are never you.
You are things some never learn.

At the summit only empty hands are found.
But the minds are palaces.
The voices become nations.

Barrow: *n. A wheelbarrow, a tool or vehicle for carrying small loads, possibly first originating in Asia ca. 100 BCE. A container particularly useful for the construction of many things.*

"They tend to be suspicious, bristly, paranoid-type people with huge egos they push around like some elephantiasis victim with his distended testicles in a wheelbarrow terrified no doubt that some skulking ingrate of a clone student will sneak into his very brain and steal his genius work."

- William S. Burroughs, *Immortality*

XXII

Who depended
Upon

An Asian
Barrow

Nearby

Strays
Beneath an aimless star

Vocabularies

I look at florid Xue Di
thinking of words I stopped using.

Gone, departed: bleak and stagnant streams,
grown limpid with moss and dying memories
of Nineveh and Nihilism.

Blasted into the oblivion of the unused page:
stoic reflections on Marcus Aurelius
and Cappucino monks.

Dreaded Mahakala no longer comes in like the Kali Yuga
to plunge his timeless hands into my heart
to fuel the cryptic mandalas and labyrinths I once
understood so well.

I can't buy a cup of coffee from the Starbucks mermaid
        with even half of my latter verses
              and a dollar in change.

Where is: my poem to commemorate the Dalai Lama's visit,
when a decade ago, I fought like that Persian lion Rustam to see him?

When was the last time I spoke of arhats and boddhisatva vows?

Melancholy creeps over me like a giant kudzu.

    I'm rotting from compromise on the vine,
    and if I don't turn it around,
    I'll be an unexploded raisin
    or pressed into some unsavory vintage
    stored in the distended corner of some discount cellar.

But as I open the papers to the limbless youths of Iraq
and broken buddhas on the Afghan plains
it's hard to take writer's block seriously.

> What is a lost word to a boy without a hand?

> What does a missing sentence mean
> to the condemned man in Congo who will die without even
> a last meal?

Despair over a dearth of words is despicable.

> To be wrapped up in semantics while semi-automatics chew apart
> the youth in the heart of our cities is ... well, I've lost the word.

But I have no right to lament, and lift my pen to write again...

Chartreuse

The color of the flamethrower
Is different from the flame

On a blazing bamboo hut
Or a charring Iraqi conscript

Who's been caught on camera
But deemed unfit for television

Lest public opinion get peeled down
Like a yellow onion on the cutting board.

A housewife from Humboldt Avenue stops into
The Shuang Cheng with her friend who loves
The scarlet lobster smothered in ginger

Marveling at the incredible array of colors
That are available today

Praising the technicians of beauty
Who paint new souls on for a pittance

Isn't it a scream, she says.
Isn't it a scream.

Outside, it has begun to snow.
And the tiny poets of the world declare it

The fingerprints of God.

Homunculus

We always want to make
Little men, playing around
In the kitchens of the gods
We made and prayed to

When midnight lightning
Could not be expressed
As a mere one plus one equation
To the Children of Oceans.

Their heirs, the Turning Wheels,
Today give snide smiles
To antique alchemy in
Favor of the clones we pray
Will surpass their aging mold,

A step short of immortal,
As righteous as the Zero.

Genesis 2020

The new ark shall be compact
The size of a Gucci suitcase:
A thousand microvials brimming
With an incriminating sampling of our genetic meandering
Since the tree of life was a sapling.

Like a magician's trick unfolded,
A babbling ocean now stares
As the genie is put back into the bottle,
On the rocks, into the waves.

A hermetic voyager
Singing a Homeric ode
Across time's elliptical odyssey.

At least until the battery
Wears out...

The Dancer Introduces One of His Aspects

I am Shiva, I am Kali,
I am the bird you never see.

With riddles infested full of dreams,
I am the corpse that pollutes the stream.

I am the angel, soot-eyed with breath of pitch.
I am your hound, found by the ditch.

I am the bait of a child, hanging in the glooms.
I am the memory of She, interred in the tomb.

My hands are the coiling tendrils of a drying jade vine,
My feet are the fires doused by the vagrant's wine.

My heart is the wheel, breaking the road.
My kiss and my spit, the gifts of my lips, the precious abode.

My ribs are the spars from which flowers grow,
My bones are the tethers the sages know.

My eyes are the conquerors who ride through the night,
My howl, the laughter of children born anew out of sight

Plunged down as a pavement for my eternal act.
You try to flee?

I am the dancer, I am the city.

Riding the 16

Forty-five minutes
is enough time to write
a small book of poems
but they never seem to come
until you're furthest away from a pen.

It must be the rhythm of the skyline:

>The faces of strangers grow more familiar
>yet quiet as a Somalian maiden at 9 A.M.
>
>A Russian tea house has gone out of business.
>
>A carniceria is offering fresh meat
>while Xieng Khouang and Saigon become neighbors
>once more, amid falling borders and empty buildings
>for the American dreamers.
>
>Porky's holds onto cold war prosperity and
>dine-in-your-car sensibilities, a neon blaze at night.
>
>The Hong Kong Noodle House has flourished since the handover.

An old German photographer laughs with me about the noise
of a Minolta at the ballet and the fall of civilization to Y2K.

He's showing me a book about comedy left at the previous stop,
chuckling at strange fortunes, quantum physics and
the clocks dotting our way.

I don't catch his name, trundling off at my stop,
wondering how people find poetry without the bus.

Labyrinth

After so many years
And all my tears I've shed,
This, at last:

After so many years
Pent up in my Maze of head and paste,
I can now say it's all "past".

After so many years
Freely clear, by my own hand,
I once more gaze upon the Sun.

After so many years
My cost: my wife, my job,
My only son.

After so many years
My prison I've made,
Simple dust.

After so many years
I can return to what I've missed
So long, and rebuild my prisons anew.

My only art that I can trust.

Barrow: *n. A pig castrated before it reaches sexual maturity.*

Two entries from the *Devil's Dictionary* of Ambrose Bierce, who mysteriously disappeared to much remark:

> "Edible, adj.: Good to eat, and wholesome to digest, as a worm to a toad, a toad to a snake, a snake to a pig, a pig to a man, and a man to a worm."

> "Youth is the true Saturnian Reign, the Golden Age on earth again, when figs are grown on thistles, and pigs betailed with whistles and, wearing silken bristles, live ever in clover, and clows fly over, delivering milk at every door, and Justice never is heard to snore, and every assassin is made a ghost and, howling, is cast into Baltimost!"

To the Pet Shop Gecko

Behind the glass,
You haven't the song

To make young girls free you.
You're no covert prince after a kiss

And you won't take flight
Like an ugly duckling.

Over a wise pig's brick house.
Sticking pitifully to this tank,

Sometimes I wish you could blink
A Morse message to Heaven

Where your silver cousins play in the
Stellar furnaces of the Dragon King.

But for now all we get is your quiet instrumental
Edited for television

Between episodes of American Idol
And Just Shoot Me

Modern Life

With its happy hours and high rises
Is hard to capture:
It's a glimpse from a paused bus
Of a classic car
Sparkling impatiently
At a red stoplight, itching
To roar off to Porky's
In the Spring
While young Hmong boys
Parked in a grimy Lexington lot
Rev their thundering import engines for
Slender brown-eyed girls slinking around
In so-sexy Frankenstein heels
Waiting for the cops in their fancy cruisers
To blink

So our race can begin

Sprawl

Sexy as the flesh warm against the grey
We exhale, touching true earth
Typically by 24 inches at a time
Except when sleeping.

Our forms half rain, half mud, half heat of day,
Half cold of night.

We're all bundled tube, incomplete orifice,
We stuff, we ram, we chew

Discontent with hollow.

There's life at stake for
Sausage City. So we don't
stop for much.

So rarely as one, as mob
We are our rubbing cells

Needing more, but not much more.
Distrusting excess mass presence over
Suspect intimacy.
--
Grimy, vein and solid, soft
Groping together before suns expire

Our mouths open as city gates,
Smooth roads lined in wet red carpet.

The Big G.

We don't say his name aloud in serious poetry.
We close our eyes and say he doesn't exist.
I am a modern eastern Peter with a mouth of denials
While the cocks crow at the rising sun.

Right next to a certain master of Jeet Kune Do,
He stood like a giant torii gate
Between my heart and the American flag.

How many people were surprised, when my words
Moved in time with my lips.

Even today, they still believe my buildings
Can't stand the test of time, crumbling
At the first sign of trouble
Like a pasty French defense
Only a swarthy legion of strangers can vindicate.

But the old boy's got stamina-
He's neck and neck with James Bond,
Trampling the Police Academies and Shakespeare plays.

Now, why should I reject this reliable radioactive lug,
Just to be taken seriously by some stiff academe
With erectile dysfunction and a bad toupee?

And in learning to love the reptile,
Perhaps we can learn to love ourselves,
Atomic halitosis and all.

Cobra

The more I think about it
The more I think

I'm going to name my first
Girl Cobra

Just to see how many
Will rush to kiss her

Expecting a belladonna flower
To explode in their mouth

Like a yellow cluster bomb
Everyone thought

Was a dud.

That's paternal instinct for you.
But I suspect I'm going to be
Overridden

By her mother,
Who loves all beautiful things.

2019 Blues

Home again?　　　　　　　　　　"Good evening!"
Ho. Me? A gain.
Jiggety jig.

To market, to market,　　　　　<< Commerce. That's our goal. Here. >>

To buy a fat hog,　　　　　　　"More Human
　　　　　　　　　　　　　　　　Than Human."

Home a gain.　　　　　　　　　*If only you could see…*
Ho: Me again…　　　　　　　　<<You've done a man's job.>>

　　　　　Jiggety Jog.
　　I. Guess. You're through, huh?

▮ was not called 'execution,' it was ▮ 'retirement.'

　　　　You're little, people[1]

1:　La gente paga, e rider vuole qua.　　　　From 1838 to 1841
　　Ridi, Pagliaccio, e ognun applaudirà!　　St. Paul, Minnesota
　　　　La Commedia è Finita!　　　　　　　　Was Pig's Eye.

From various suspect traditions:
A Hmong shaman in the 20th century requested a pig's jaw.
Chinese and Italians? Rumored to eat every part of a pig but the squeal.
Tonight, it rained. No one could stop it, especially not a poor beat cop.

Legion

Our true names?
Power.
Possession,
Our aim.

So many means to read this.
Foreign. American. Demon.

Swine before a pearl-filled sea?

We die. For many reasons.
Good book, Equality,
Liberty, Fraternity,
Out of many, one.

We yearn to be free.
This, our unity.

Zhū Bājiè

Tian Peng Yuan Shuai was
The honored Grand Admiral of 80,000,
Marshall of the Heavenly River.

Under his proud hand,
The enemies of the empire met doom by sea,
Sinking beyond eye and history, or dying in mud, forgotten mayflies.
To each their duty. Names for the victorious only.

What his foes fought and died for, their societies of tools and song,
Could be of no concern. Only tomorrow and blood, blade and command.

For centuries there were no Chinese autobiographies.
Only their commentaries on the words of war and state
Applied.

Paper and ink were holy here.

All he truly saw, lost in the bureaucracy of testimonies.
During his final peach banquet among the heavens, Chang'e,
Goddess of the moon,
Was a beauteous guest before the splendors he preserved.

> Who would not be a fool before her?
> Who would not risk all for her attentions?

To her, he was just another drunken butcher the empress rebuked.

In apology, the admiral, abashed, resigned.
To earth descending, to be a better legend.

    Later on some savage isle,
    The Lord of the Flies makes a meal of a boar's head,
    Knowing nothing of Tian Peng Yuan Shuai,
    The lives he ended or the lives he led.

One December morning,
A poet waits for April in Minneapolis
Thinking of a pretty girl, a moon, a pig.

Barrow: *n. A count of forty threads in the warp or chain of woolen cloth.*

"In a giant, empty decaying building which had once housed thousands, a single TV set hawked its wares to an uninhabited room.

The ownerless ruin had, before World War Terminus, been tended and maintained. Here had been the suburbs of San Francisco, a short ride by monorail rapid transit; the entire peninsula chattered like a bird tree with life and opinions and complaints, and now the watchful owners had either died or migrated to a colony world. Mostly the former; it had been a costly war…"

-Do Androids Dream of Electric Sheep?
Philip K. Dick

Minotaur

There is nothing behind the red silk cape of the matador.
If you're looking for the man,
Look to the side.

        Charging furious, a raging coal
        Caught in the moment

For Spanish swordsmen
Wrapped up in an inevitable scene

Switching places with his killer.

        Something dies within him,
        Not knowing why

Reconsidering Gordian

What have you done?

In a single stroke, what have you undone?

Brute Philistine, you were no Goliath
But in a moment of pragmatic impatience...

        Words fail.

For centuries I could not disprove you.

In a decade of troubled dreams,
You still won, every time.

I was a fool to pin a kingdom to a knot.

I am a villain for the lesson I allow you to teach.

Just as well you never met the Sphinx,
Drunkard.

For the Friend Who Will Never Read This

Your hair,

a splash of ink on a pale page
a bound loop of
particolored thread
for a paj ntaub
laced with the scent of flowers
I cannot name.

On an Autumn couch
reading this
after work
you are a

soft brush laced with razors
no one ███ about
except me.

During work,
I'm writing.

Libertree

The tree of liberty devours the loyal
Grinding them between burning flag teeth and a ton of open doors.
Blue lakes formed in the footprints of Babe
While the trail of tears formed a bloody river.

Washington had a thing for breaking cherry trees and raising hemp
That was good for strong ropes to bind us all together
In a frenetic world of neckties and necessities.

No one knows the names of Afghan heroes or Hmong veterans
Whose fathers raised opium crops now littered with landmines.

Few can tell you where Russia is, even after fifty years
Of cold wars in tropical nations they "never vacationed in, personally."
They would be unable to tell you how many of our allies are
In an impossible debt, negotiating a cost-effective betrayal.
But they can tell you about "Friends" and Miss October.

Miscellaneous documents outlining
Illiterate farmers with $200 anti-tank weapons
Have surfaced to air our missile mania,
A culture where no one sees the irony
Of naming a million-dollar cruise missile
After a tomahawk, while defanged reservations cope
With under-funded schools.

People laugh as immigrants report stories of American giants
Who press you beneath their green thumbs stained with dollars
When it's time to eat.

Cannibalized ideas and epics lay exhausted, scattered apple-seeds
In urban canyons formed by alien policies of war and leverage.
And a great love of sequels.

Half of the nation has never seen an orchard,
Only the recycled city papers
They are being ignored in as usual.

Somehow, the Cubans managed to preserve
The purity of baseball and cigars
While we still can't imagine the rules to Canadian curling,
Despite our open borders.

And strangely, when a laughing yellow cab driver
Who was a former engineer from Iraq tells me about
US chemical weapons and acid rain,
I'm just not as surprised as I wish I could be.

His last words rang like a cracked bell outside
Of a smoking capitol of conspiracies:

"When there's a new war, watch.
A refreshing new ethnic restaurant will open in your neighborhood
Soon…"

Lady Xoc

Jesus marimba, lady, your noble rite
Leaves me with nightmares.
Jack the Ripper and Doctor Lecter
Have nothing on your offers
Of paper, blood and flame
From your well-traveled tongue.

The taste of midnight thorns from
Fragrant Yaxchilan shrubbery
Are regal semaphore flags
Fluttering for the coldest heavens.

Shield Jaguar with his raging torch covertly
Averts his stony gaze from
The barbed stingray tail dangling within
Your delicate hands, struggling not to wince.

"It is the smoke," he mutters.
To blanch: Unbecoming of a warrior king.

My department says I'm an ethnocentric brute
Who understands nothing
Of the demands of power among the Maya.

My American judgments have no place
Amid your holy incantations, and I will be
Ostracized like Socrates for suggesting

Our First Ladies should be grateful
Things turned out this way
And not the other.

But you have little to say about anything,
The curve of your stone lips cryptic as the maiden
In Michelangelo's mirror, tied to a thread
More painful than any Gordian knot.

Everything Belongs to the Spider

I
have book lungs for your knives
      I circle on the thinnest trap line
Gaze eight times before brunch
              Upon the desiccated casts I left behind

              Awaiting meals like
An antsy kid for a campfire ghost…

Regrettably, this silky web
      I wish would lasso   a rose-haired sunset

Snags
only
shriveled
dried shades
and pests
each
night.

      But it will be mine,
someday.

Severances

For your end we have so much blade
To sever cord of dream and body.
Harden an edge sufficiently. Clip.
Be still.

One proper stroke. A lifetime. There.
The rest awaits.

Sheer, the cliffs of old you scaled.
Certain, we finite in our tasks, our days:
Someday, none shall need of clothing.
One day, we fates shall eye our own,

Our slender threads entwined
With every story known.

Leveled without witness. Without peer.

Loom

Build a frame for tapestries,
Rouse we, these hands of stories,
These eyes for the hidden gazing!

A loom in silence? Nothing comes.
A loom alive, might bring a bolt,
A suit, a sin, a magic carpet for some.

Arachne, Ariadne, Aladdin, Inktomi, Anansi.
Each laughs, bound in their own way.
Some to vanity, to wit, to beauty,
Like fierce Circe among her swine
And incantations,

Challenging our shouldered world to be
Not practical banality but labyrinthine,
Amazing!

Shuttle

I bear a thread.

Here, I convey by certain route,
My domain, my colorful road of cloth
That might array a king or waif.
My life is repetition, passing and binding.
Warp and woof.

What arrives by shuttle
May change your life
Like a star you want to touch,

A robe of riddles you want to unravel,
A yarn the age repeats for dreaming butterflies
          And a distant sound of thunder.

A Sum of Threads

Lost stories abound, loitering like lusty mules,
Ebullient commerce of buck, babe and gamble.

To lose is the gain of the unknown.
Here,
In the shadow of the good earth,

The whitest pearl is still a single hard grain.

I greet you, weaver between your thin red webs.
When I'm not looking, I know, like a Harry Harlow monkey

You're secretly the wind of Texas,
A lion in Chicago, a hungry oyster on rainy 9th and Hennepin
Or a drowsy parrot in Saline of curious hue.

I want to take you home, kin, but we never know our place.

               We laughgh with lighght, high above the type

Oh, who swear, by their loud traditions and trajectories apparent
"Connections can seal," a cad's roar with lips of misplaced baggage.

    They hypnotize the sun like a Mississippi
    Rebus,
    A crow, no, a raven, no, a rook flapping to Pluto or some palace
    Nameless,

    Victorious, a halo, a tramp pyre. Free. Transforming
    An answer waiting to be buried, rebelling, uncaging
    Defiant, you lovely want of mine.

Clothing me, a ray, a tapestry of dreamers, a flag adopted.

Tie: A Knot's Perspective

To tie is to connect,
To live as more than mere falling leaf
Broke from branch to earth and mold.

If I talk of one thing, I am not.
I bend to tangle and hold.
Pull or cut, I release.

Who are we but the wrapping around choices,
Thoughts and dreams, the occasional virus,
Some dust and fluid, a speck of desire and spirit?

Rig our bonds like sailors or cowboys,
Scouts or tailors, lash selves to cultures,
Masts of meaning, one of many cosmic misty toys

    Discovering velcro.

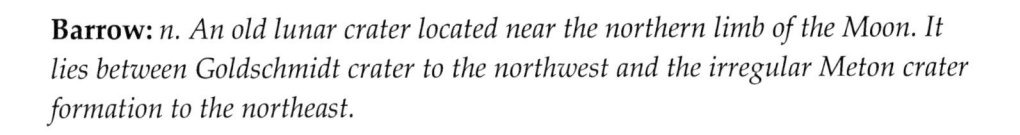

Barrow: *n. An old lunar crater located near the northern limb of the Moon. It lies between Goldschmidt crater to the northwest and the irregular Meton crater formation to the northeast.*

"When a finger points to the moon, the imbecile looks at the finger."
– Chinese Proverb.

"What, you want, do you, to come unawares,
Sweeping the church up for first morning-prayers,
And find a poor devil has ended his cares
At the foot of your rotten-runged rat-riddled stairs?
Do I carry the moon in my pocket?"
- Robert Browning

"I only know two pieces; one is 'Clair de Lune' and the other one isn't"
- Victor Borge

Acts of Confession

Wanderer of the night
I Am
Simpler than said before
I strip off this form
So frail and hesitant
I cleanse the sin from my bones
Dry the sweat and tears of my toil
I take out my heart. Let it breathe
Fresh Air.

Moon is my witness
As the transformation begins,
If slowly,
To restore once more:

>That which was lost
>So long before

A Little Bat

flutters by on the beach
at noon,
a tiny klutz clutching
frantically at the wind.

    She doesn't know if
    she is a bird
    or a mouse.

In antique Indochine
she was mocked by
hoary men for her indecision

  and today, even her
loving brothers and sisters
  think she's gone mad as a loon

    uncertain if she is coming home
    or leaving

  for an illicit rendezvous
with a sleeping moon
    beneath winking canopies of green
  no man has ever seen.

Mischief in the Heavens

Here they go again:
Time with her pinwheel face

And Space, whose titanic feet
Stand tippy-toe on cesium atoms

To peer over the fourth wall
For the sacred cookie jar of the gods.

How they frown to find it stuffed
With human souls that taste like carob.

It's like Karma coming by with another damn fruitcake.

The Spirit Catches You,
and You Get Body Slammed

I came to Missoula to ask him
About the inner workings of ua neeb.
To understand the symbolic significance of split horns
And spirit horses who trace their noble smoky path
To turns of an auspicious moon above ancient Qin.

My tape recorder at the ready,
My fountain pen freshly filled with indigo ink,
My ears, my eyes, my heart:
All were humbly waiting for
The wise shaman's words
To impart to the next generation
Of youths who sought this fading voice.

He spoke, and my interpreter said:
"Who's your favorite wrestler?"

I wasn't certain I'd heard properly.

"Grandpa wants to know who your favorite wrestler is."
My interpreter turned back to the shaman, speaking Hmong.

Rising with a stately elder's grace, the shaman confidently said:
"Randy Macho Man Savage!" and struck a macho pose.

Smiling, he then offered me a cup of hot coffee.
I was too stunned to say anything more
For the rest of the afternoon.

Years later, I still have dreams of shining Shee Yee
Smashing writhing demons into blue turnbuckles,
Watching next to a hundred smiling shamans in the audience.

Dragon Jazz

Woke up and thought I was Moses.
Went to bed and knew I was worm food.

Worms feed the fish that might become dragons.
Words feed the men that might become monsters.

In the mirror I face the monster I'm becoming.
In the streets I face the monsters who became me!

To find myself, my teachers said look to the past,

And my past told me to find my teachers by looking
Straight at the concrete center of

      Then and Tomorrow.

I went to the West chasing its tale.
I went to the East shooting at the moon.

I ran into God walking his secret dogs:
He asked, "How do you like it here so far?"
My answer was close to:

      "Well enough that I'll stick around for tomorrow.
      Thanks for asking."

Tempus Fugit

Time flies, but it's going in circles too,
A celestial hula hoop
For a shimmying deity's tiniest toys
Pinned to obscure orbits.

Plus ça change, plus c'est la même chose,

Racing at full tilt like an old Spanish cavalier
On a windmill course to the other end of the start line
Grinding golden grain beneath her giant feet!

Who threw this disc into the air in the first place?
The sun a starter pistol, the moon a stopwatch,
Our eyes an imperfect witness

                        Consistently blinking before the finish line is crossed.

Soap

Tiny mouths of the world, how you dread
The floating bars in a mother's hand as they
Are offered before the cleansing water, and foam

Without a hint of the ash and lye
        They're made from.

***

We think: milky white bubbles signify some great purity
Just shy of perfection against a lab-coat's chuckling scales.

      That faint whiff of perfume left on the skin
      Means we have journeyed to some higher state,

And the resentful tongue will be thankful when reflective
In some long-boned future

As it is washed into nothing like a vanishing moon
Devoured by a malachite frog hungry for the heavens.

***

Scrubbing and scouring, my Hera, your eyes
Never did find those four-letter words the boy muttered.

Sitting by your righteous hearth in your splendor,
I regret to inform you:
His malady has spread with age, despite your damn remedies!

***

In the news today, they say antibacterial soap
May in fact promote the birth of wily superbacteria
Whose monstrous nature will thrust us into the sterile arms

Of titanic pharmaceutical companies
Who specialize in slaying such tiny hydras,
For a price our children may be unable to afford.

The Fifth Wish

Thus far? Universally
Unfulfilled. But the most

Reflective and wise
Draws from:

[1] The testing.
Typically small and wasted,
Planted seeds of awe upon delivery.

[2] Grandiose designs.
Undone by many a devil's details
Scratched out in red ink: "Rewards? Regrets."

[3] Folly peaks.
Rules now learned, the clumsy tongue strives,
Recognizes precision's value to desire. Still fails.

[4] Undoes everything.
We return to our faceless world, as it was, but wiser.
But not so wise

To not still seek what we cannot have. [5]

Insomniacafe

If God with his hundred sacred names
must caper about
like a young child full of infinity
hiding among a blade of field grass,
grey cathedral cornerstones
or the wizened hands of a stranger in Calcutta
overcome with kindness
in a cosmic game
of peek-a-boo,
how can he hold a grudge
against those honest enough to say
"I don't know if I've really seen him lately?"

Lording over a cup of cappuccino
like an Italian monk on watch at midnight,
I wonder briefly if the faithful will have to sit
in a corner of paradise for a while
for perjury.

With another sip,
eyes wide as Daruma
or some crazed cartoon cat,
I wonder if I'll ever get to sleep this way...

Swallowing the Moon

Some see an anonymous man or a thief of sheep.
Some a goddess like Hina-i-ka-malama or Chang'e.
Perhaps a princess of rabbits or a magician's jealous head,
Her face painted with bells.
Cain.
A criminal from the Book of Numbers.
A cook. A witch. A home for the dead among those stones.

A zoo hungers
With bellies for cosmic lights:
Nak, lung, serpentine Bakunawa.
Wolves, frogs and old gods seeking a bite!

We chase with fireworks, bold arrows, bullets, hoots,
Our clamor of mortals who wish to journey to heaven and return
Mischievous ravens and spiders, master marksmen and demigods.
Defenders, uncontested, unsung.

Become more than lucky monkeys with fire and pens.

Hey, Einstein

> "God does not play dice with the universe."
> - Albert Einstein

Playing dice in God's universe
Doesn't get you any closer to him.
Understanding craps
Does as much good as knowing old maids.
Random acts of kindness, like one-armed bandits
Have an uncertain payoff.
You can go fish, reach 21 and hit me,
But divine conversations occur
With all of the frequency of a royal straight flush
On a blue moon in the Year of the Dragon
During your final hour on death row, waiting for a pardon.

Unfortunately, beating those odds only happens if you play.

Lunacy

Oh, lady of cycle and changing face.
Huntress, wise and crafty, timeless so!
I kiss you with lips of drying ink
Thinking you'll remember I sought you
By the sea, among the pages of earth, within skulls

And the senseless things who do not know
Like a city without myth,

A wild heart of incense. My eye afire.
A lost marble rolling towards a forgiving ocean.

VI.

q. what book would you take with you on a deserted island?

"My own. If I'm not writing the kind of book I'd take with me, what kind of writing am I doing?"
-Somnouk Silosoth.

"I'd take along a copy of the dictionary—which, as comedian Steven Wright noted, is sort of a poem about everything. From this book one can invent virtually all others, given time."
-Eric Lorberer.

"How To Build A Boat."
-Steven Wright.

How to Build a Boat

I. Arrival Upon This Island, Earth.

>How did we get
>To "Who?"
>
>To "Where
>Are we?"
>
>To "We are."
>
>The rivers of death, myth lead to the living:
>The Nile, the Ganges, the Mekong, the Styx and Sanzu.
>The Mississippi of legend, the Amazons of dreamers.
>To oceans of mazes as simple as every open eye.

II. The Proven Tools To See Tomorrow.

Don't panic.

You will fail if you don't remember arrogant Icarus-
All your tools, naught but icons of ingenuity and not true keys,
Defying ambitions of escape among even the most fertile forests.

Antique monoliths wager you'll be stone before long.
Nevermore among the wonders of Paris, Lane Xang or D.C.
If chaos trumps memory and your hearth becomes an abstraction.

>Fret if you've implements but not will.

Castaway, you need not fashion the Titanic or the Ark of song,
Some vessel more elaborate than Kon Tiki
For your humble odyssey as a letter in the word of Life.

Craft an even keel, a sturdy hull and rudder,
The guiding tiller lashed by vine, weed or bark.
Be raven, not roach.

        Open Pandora's box now. Unleash hope.

III. Food for Thought.

"I am what I am."
Thus spake the sea salt and the First.

    You, fighting sea hags, despair, vultures
    Who feast upon those surrendered, smashed minnows
    Here, among the wild things?

Prevail.
Watch astral bodies tremble, with their puzzles of love and names.

    See where you are, creature of the creator.
    Use your resources wisely: mind, body. Without and within.
    Remember and draw from the unwritten libraries of life.
    Vanquish fear, the mind killer, a little obliterator.
    Improve your conditions by inches, by days, by miles and dreams.
    Value living and liberation.
    Escape.

Occupy space with no intention of staying,
Burn to reach another star someday.

Even if you must hunt flying pigs, electric sheep.

IV. Stranding Ends.

"It is finished."
> These words?
> Not necessarily the end,
> The beginning of the end,
> But perhaps a beginning's end.

All worlds? Impermanent.
The sound of a bell, the color of a flower, prosperity and pride.
They, a spring dream, the mighty fallen, dust for the wind so brief.

But the cosmos renews by its curious turns of storm and wave,
Cycle and forms, shedding shells and skins, seeds and meaning.
A monkey chase of mermaids.

> We cross our pyrrhic Rubicons, our Potomacs,
> Face decisive Bach Dang and Dan-No-Ura.
>
> Dare to begin.
> Find your song, start singing.

Even if we must die,
We are no penned swine of inglorious spot.
We rise from our knees against monsters, we carry on against rot!

True beginnings uncertain, true endings uncertain,
But today will lead to tonight.
For now, that is enough.

> Like young Scheherazade, we have something to continue,
> As tomorrow and tomorrow and tomorrow
> Oh, may become another country.

V. Finding Your Way.

We, hewn stars by stars escape. Hoka hey!
Four hundred and thirty light years away, Polaris guides steadily.
Make your way like Nemo or Zhang He.

> Traverse mosaic, a nautilus, a lotus: Bob, if not home, to destiny.
> Remember to smile when you glimpse another soul:
> Alas, unlikely some guiding Beatrice ending your comedy,
> Doubtful a pious albatross of good omen wandering but not lost,
> Or divine talking tygers appraising hungrily.
> Probably only a tongue, a free eye, a strange hand. It will do.
> This moment is an anchor or a stair. A pearl or a cold locker.
> Be vigilant, accept gracefully as Job, defy the tyranny of the sea

> > Who would swallow your story,
> >   Easily, anonymously.
>
> > What are you starving for?
>
> > Vi Veri Vniversum Vivus Vici!

VI. The Self As Somewhere To Go.

I am not a number.
I am free. I will not be pushed, filed or indexed
To die some rotten cabbage resigned. I shall be defiant as Papillion,
"No Man" escaping, an unrepentant butterfly from Devil's Isle.

The trick to living forever is simple: Don't die.

> > Whether stranded by Chiron or Alpha Centauri,
> > Frogtown or the Island of Lost Misfit Children
> > I will be free as Sisyphus or a lad's ingenious genie
> > Who denies no exit with a smile imagined happy.
> > The stranger in a strange land, unbound

> Even if I must turn into a sea wolf, a magic nak,
> A sovereign of flying monkeys,
> A lion racing the moon
> Or Drake among the tempests or the laughing bird men.

Remember me - if at all - not as lost.

Rejoice: A way a lone a last a loved a long arrive

About the Author

Bryan Thao Worra was born in 1973 in Laos during the Laotian civil war.

He came to the US at six months old, adopted by a civilian pilot flying in Laos. Today, Bryan Thao Worra has a unique impact on contemporary art and literature within the Lao, Hmong, Asian American and the transcultural adoptee communities, particularly in the Midwest. In 2003, Thao Worra reunited with his biological family after 30 years during his first return to Laos.

A poet, short story writer, playwright and essayist, his prolific work appears internationally in numerous anthologies, magazines and newspapers, including *Bamboo Among the Oaks, Contemporary Voices of the East, Tales of the Unanticipated, Illumen, Astropoetica, Outsiders Within, Dark Wisdom, Hyphen, Journal of the Asian American Renaissance, Bakka, Whistling Shade, Tripmaster Monkey, Asian American Press* and *Mad Poets of Terra*. He is the author of **On the Other Side of the Eye** and **Winter Ink**.

Thao Worra curated numerous readings and exhibits of Lao and Hmong American art including **Emerging Voices** (2002), **The 5 Senses Show** (2002), **Lao'd and Clear** (2003), **Giant Lizard Theater** (2005), **Re:Generations** (2005), and **The Un-Named Series** (2007). He speaks nationally at colleges, schools and community institutions including the Loft Literary Center, Intermedia Arts, the Center for Independent Artists and the Minneapolis Institute of Art. In 2009 he received an NEA Fellowship In Literature for his poetry.

Thao Worra is working on his next books and several personal projects including efforts to reconnect expatriate Lao artists and writers with their contemporary counterparts in Laos following over 30 years of isolation.

ACKNOWLEDGEMENTS

A Hmong Goodbye, Poems Niederngasse, January/February, 2005
Genesis 2020, Whistling Shade, Summer, 2002
Here, the River Haunt, Whistling Shade, Fall, 2008.
Hey, Einstein, The Big G., Mischief in the Heavens, Defenestration Magazine, 2004
Homonculus, Soap Tales of the Unanticipated #28, 2006
Insomniacafe, Real Eight View, October, 2004
Modern Life, To the Petshop Gecko, Unarmed, 2002.
My Autopsy, Thank You, Journal of the Asian American Renaissance, Winter 2001
Sprawl, The Fifth Wish, Still Life, Northography.Com, 2008
*Tetragrammaton,*Stirring, December 2003.
The Spirit Catches You and You Get Body Slammed, Paj Ntaub Voice, Summer 2003
Today's Special at the Shuang Cheng, Mid-American Poetry Review, 2004.
What Tomorrow Takes Away, Pedestal Magazine, November, 2004

Khop Jai Lai!